The AI Failure Handbook

The Ultimate Guide to Screwing Up Your AI Transformation

Dr. David R. Hardoon

ISBN: 978-981-94-6444-9

DEDICATION

"I may not have gone where I intended to go, but I think I have ended up where I needed to be." — Douglas Adams

This book is dedicated, with the most earnest irony, to every executive, manager, data scientist, change agent, governance committee member, and procurement officer who has ever dreamed, truly, deeply, passionately of making a difference.

However small that difference may turn out to be.

Your passion is real.

The Page Is Left Intentionally Blank

Should you require content here, please submit Form BP-47 (Request for Non-Blankness) in triplicate to the Transformation Task Force. Expected response time: 6-9 months.

CONTENTS

This Page Has Been Left Intentionally Blank

After review and approval by the Blank Page Governance Committee. Version 1.2 | Approved: Never | Risk Level: Acceptable (subject to further wordsmithing).

ACKNOWLEDGMENTS

We extend our sincerest thanks to the following inanimate co-conspirators, without whom this handbook would never have achieved such magnificent futility.

To the photocopier that jammed with theatrical timing.
To the calendar that mysteriously doubled every meeting.
To the email server that delivered only at 11:58 p.m.
To the rogue stapler that declined anything beyond 3 pages.
To the kettle that boiled at every moment of near success.
To the meeting-room light that flickered in perfect sabotage.
To the left-handed mouse that appeared uninvited.
To the immortal coffee stain on the carpet.
To the lift that resolutely stopped at floor 7.

Our families raised a single weary eyebrow and inquired about the wine.

And to you, dear reader: well played. You have joined the noble fellowship of objects that quietly understand success is vastly overrated.

We couldn't have failed nearly so well without them.

The Page Is Left Intentionally Blank

Don't worry, we've scheduled three workshops to discuss filling it.

1 FORWARD

Welcome, dear reader, to the only AI book you probably shouldn't forward to your CEO.

Everyone else is still publishing the same tired liturgy: "10 Steps to AI Success", "The Responsible AI Framework", "How We Deployed Generative AI and Saved Millions" (complete with suspiciously precise numbers and accompanying slide decks). Glossy case studies. Bullet-point recipes. Triumphalist quotes from leaders who are either exceptionally lucky or exceptionally gifted at selective storytelling.

Meanwhile the numbers remain brutally honest.

Up to 95% of AI initiatives fail to deliver meaningful business value. Most pilots never graduate from PowerPoint to production. Organisations proudly declaring they have been "doing AI" for years still quietly classify themselves as "in experimentation mode". Budgets vanish into infrastructure, governance theatre, and training modules that nobody actually finishes. And yet the conference circuit is still packed with people selling success.

Something is clearly amiss.

After two decades of watching the same film on repeat, expert systems, neural nets, big data, machine learning, deep learning, now generative everything, the pattern is no longer subtle. The organisations that reliably underperform aren't stupid. They aren't lazy. They aren't even unlucky.

They are, with impressive consistency, following a very particular set of recipes.

Not the recipes for success, obviously. The other ones. The elegant, repeatable, almost beautiful ways to ensure that multimillion-dollar transformations end up as line items in next year's "lessons learned" slide deck.

So here we are.

Instead of yet another earnest guide to "winning with AI", I have decided to do the opposite on purpose. In this handbook I will lovingly document the precise moves that, when executed with even moderate competence, are almost guaranteed to keep your organisation firmly in the 80–95% club, the vast majority that talks a good game about AI but quietly fails to move the needle on revenue, cost, customer experience, or competitive position.

This is not a cry for help. This is not passive-aggressive consulting. This is reverse psychology with a straight face.

If you are the kind of leader who melts when confronted with uncomfortable mirrors, close the book now. If you believe your organisation is already different, that your governance is lean, your data is pristine, your culture is psychologically safe, and your pilots are quietly delivering eight-figure value, wonderful. Put this down and go back to your quarterly review.

But if, even for a moment, you suspect that some of these

patterns might look uncomfortably familiar… well, perhaps that flicker of recognition is useful. These patterns are not unique to any one organisation or role; they are repeated industry wide.

The satire is deliberate. The humour is dark. The provocation is pointed. The intent, however, is dead serious.

This handbook owes a quiet, ironic debt to a genuine predecessor: the *Simple Sabotage Field Manual* (Strategic Services Field Manual No. 3), published in January 1944 by the Office of Strategic Services (OSS), the wartime forerunner of the CIA.

Declassified in 2008, that slim booklet taught ordinary citizens in occupied territories how to subtly cripple enemy operations through everyday incompetence: refer everything to committees, insist on channels, haggle over wording, advocate endless caution, question jurisdiction at every turn.

It was never meant for peacetime corporates. Yet here we are in the present, watching AI transformations grind to a halt under eerily similar tactics, committees that never decide, "responsible" governance that strangles momentum, "alignment" meetings that go nowhere. The OSS saboteurs didn't invent corporate dysfunction; they simply codified what already worked so well.

I am not here to sell you frameworks. I am not here to tell you how to succeed. I am here to show you, chapter by merciless chapter, exactly how most organisations ensure they do not, often by following techniques that have been field-tested since 1944.

By cataloguing the most reliable failure formulas with affection and precision, I hope to achieve three things:

1. Make you laugh (because if you can't laugh at

corporate AI theatre, you will cry).

2. Make you wince (because recognition hurts more than denial).

3. Plant the tiniest seed of doubt that maybe, just maybe, avoiding these elegant disasters is the closest thing to a cheat code that actually exists.

Read it. Recognise it. Laugh at it. And, if the humour lands just right, perhaps quietly rethink one or two things before the next budget cycle.

Try not to recognize too much of your own organisation in it. And if you do, well, any resemblance to true events, living persons, or actual organisations, living or dead, is entirely coincidental and without merit. This is a work of satire. No CxOs were harmed in the writing of this manifesto. Probably.

Because the real joke isn't that AI is hard. The real joke is that so many of us keep doing the same things that make it impossible… and then act surprised when it stays impossible.

Enjoy the handbook. The mirror is open.

Now turn the page.

We're about to get specific.

— Dr. David R. Hardoon

(And remember always carry a towel. You never know when you'll need to put it over your head. If you can't see them, they can't see you.)

2 JUST DO AI™ AND NEVER ASK "WHY" BECAUSE WHY WOULD YOU? WE ALREADY KNOW BEST (AND 95% OF PILOTS NOD IN AGREEMENT)

"Many men go fishing all of their lives without knowing that it is not fish they are after."

— *Henry David Thoreau*

You didn't begin with a customer experience that kept the CEO awake at night. You didn't begin with a cost leak that was quietly bleeding millions. You didn't even begin with a hypothesis worth the dignity of being disproved.

Worse, you began with a very comfortable set of assumptions about why things were (or weren't) happening. You assumed you already understood the customer. You assumed you knew why retention was slipping, why conversion was flat, why costs were creeping up. You assumed the problem was obvious… and all that was missing was AI.

Did anyone ever pause to ask the only question that

actually matters: "Do we actually know, or understand, the customer?"

Of course not. That would have slowed everything down.

Even more deliciously, many of you inherited a set of revenue targets and headcount-reduction goals from a predecessor who may or may not still be in the building (or the industry). Those numbers were written in PowerPoint two fiscal years ago, blessed in a strategy offsite, and now sit on your shoulders like an inherited family curse.

Common sense would suggest challenging their viability. Common sense would ask: "Are these targets still realistic given the market shift / competitor moves / macroeconomic headwinds / talent reality?"

But common sense is slow. Common sense is awkward. Common sense requires uncomfortable conversations with people who are no longer around to defend their original math.

So instead of challenging the targets, you reach for the one thing that promises to magically close any gap between ambition and reality:

AI.

Not as a carefully scoped amplifier of existing capabilities. Not as a tool to test a revised hypothesis about customer behaviour. No, as the universal solvent that will dissolve the inconvenient distance between last year's slide deck and this year's P&L.

Failure Guidebook Technique #1 – The Inherited Curse Lock-In

1. Loudly declare "We need AI to hit those targets."

2. Never, ever revisit the assumptions behind the numbers.
3. Treat any suggestion to challenge the targets as "negative thinking" or "lack of ownership."
4. When the CFO quietly asks, "Are we sure these numbers are still valid?", reply: "We're exploring AI options to bridge the gap." The room exhales. The meeting moves on. The curse lives.

Phase 1: The Tool-First Frenzy The business side is quietly, uncomfortably aware that it doesn't actually know what it wants. The customer is a black box. The root causes are murky. The inherited targets feel increasingly detached from reality.

But admitting that out loud is career-limiting.

So instead of saying "We're not sure what the real problem is," the organisation says: "We need to explore AI capabilities."

The surest way to ensure Technology happily jumps in; remain deliberately vague. Technology, bless its enthusiastic heart, hears the bat-signal and comes running.

Vendors are summoned. RFPs are issued with heroic vagueness. Sandboxes are spun up. Licences are acquired with the solemnity of a peace treaty.

Suddenly the calendar fills with demos: multimodal agents that can "revolutionise everything," platforms promising "seamless enterprise integration" and, crucially, "dramatic productivity gains."

The business nods along politely, secretly relieved that someone else is driving. Technology, meanwhile, is thrilled. Finally, a chance to buy (or worse, build) something shiny that might magically rescue the targets.

Failure Guidebook Technique #2 – The Verbal Diarrhoea Shield When the glimmer of a "wrong" path appears (someone from the business dares to ask "But how does this actually help our customer retention?"), unleash a torrent of technological verbal diarrhoea until the business person's eyes glaze over and they think: "I have no idea what they just said, it sounds extremely complicated, and therefore it must be important. Better back off and let them handle it."

Phase 2: The Internal AI Bonanza Parallel to the vendor parade comes the glorious internal construction project. A new AI Centre of Excellence is stood up (reporting, naturally, to the CTO). Titles are rebranded with cyberpunk flair. Hackathon calendars are published with military precision. Internal "AI playgrounds" are launched with town-hall fanfare.

Failure Guidebook Technique #3 – The Perpetual Re-org Shield Rebrand aggressively every quarter. Schedule regular organisational changes so clarity remains a long-forgotten urban legend. You absolutely do not want even a glimpse of organisational clarity and focus to execute.

Phase 3: The Pilot Explosion & The Menu-Flipping Ritual And then the pilots arrive. They sprout like mushrooms after rain. Each pilot is presented with breathless enthusiasm: "Look what the model can do!"

Until someone dares to ask: "So… what problem are you actually trying to solve here?"

The answer, delivered with absolute sincerity and zero self-awareness, is always some variant of: "Oh, show me what problems you've solved. We'll see if any of them match what we need."

Failure Guidebook Technique #4 – The Flip When

asked for the problem, immediately flip the menu. The logical way to discover your organisation's highest-leverage opportunity is obviously to browse a random catalogue of AI party tricks until one coincidentally matches a real pain point.

And sometimes, miraculously, someone does exclaim: "Yes! Yes! THAT is exactly my problem!"

Everyone cheers. Another tick in the "AI initiatives launched" column.

The Immediate-ROI Delusion Layer on top of this the final, exquisite contradiction: "We need immediate, quantifiable ROI from these initiatives, and we need it to hit the targets."

Pro tip for perfect contradiction: Loudly demand quick wins and payback periods while quietly refusing to touch the painful layer that would actually deliver them.

The One Truth That Everyone Pretends Not to Know AI is not about AI. AI is an amplifier. It has no intrinsic value. It creates value only when ruthlessly pointed at something that already matters, and that something must be rooted in genuine customer understanding, not comfortable assumptions.

When you begin with the tool and go hunting for problems that happen to fit the tool, you are not doing strategy. You are doing technological tourism.

"The major difference between a thing that might go wrong and a thing that cannot possibly go wrong is that when a thing that cannot possibly go wrong goes wrong it usually turns out to be impossible to get at and repair." — Douglas Adams

Your move, transformation architects. The hype train has left the station. Don't bother checking the destination. We're doing AI™.

After all this is a failure handbook, so always, but absolutely always, start with the technology. Everything else will fall into place.

3 GOVERNANCE AS PERFORMANCE ART – HOW TO STRANGLE INNOVATION WITH 47 APPROVAL LAYERS (WHILE CALLING IT "RESPONSIBLE AI")

"That's no ordinary rabbit. That's the most foul, cruel, and bad-tempered rodent you ever set eyes on."

— *Monty Python and the Holy Grail*

Governance, oh governance.

It begins with the noblest of intentions: we must be responsible. AI is powerful. AI is dangerous. AI could, if left unchecked, do unspeakable things, like accidentally generating a slightly sarcastic email or recommending a discount that costs six cents more than planned.

No one in their right mind disagrees. Which is precisely why the sentence is so lethal.

Once "responsible AI" is uttered in the boardroom, the rest unfolds with the slow, majestic inevitability of a funeral procession in a snowstorm.

Committee Everything to Death

The first commandment of elegant sabotage: if something might possibly matter, refer it to a committee.

Not one committee. Multiple overlapping committees. Committees that must meet sequentially. Committees whose minutes must be approved by other committees.

The golden rule is simple: never establish anything resembling a clear risk tolerance framework. Do not, under any circumstances, agree on what constitutes "acceptable risk." Do not publish a one-page risk appetite statement that says "We are willing to accept X level of error rate in Y context because the upside is Z."

Why would you? That would allow people to actually cross the road.

Instead, keep risk tolerance deliberately ambiguous, subjective, and emotionally charged. When someone asks, "Is this low enough risk to proceed?", respond with: "We need to think carefully about the downstream implications." "We need to ensure full alignment across all stakeholder groups." "We need further input from Legal / Ethics / Privacy."

The road never gets crossed. The chicken stands there forever, paralysed by the possibility that the other side might contain unforeseen reputational tail risk.

Double Standards: A Rule for Thee and a Rule for Me

Consistency is the enemy of good sabotage.

Make sure every team, every function, every geography operates under its own bespoke interpretation of "responsible." Marketing can run a generative campaign in production because "it's only creative copy." Legal can experiment with contract summarisation because "it's internal." But the operations team that wants to optimise a single supply-chain decision? That requires the full 47-layer gauntlet, three external audits, and a signed affidavit from the Chief Risk Officer's second cousin.

The crowning achievement is the grandfathering loophole. When, miraculously, a prototype actually works and starts delivering value, declare it "too late to unwind." "It's already in limited production." "We've collected real user feedback." "Unwinding would disrupt the business."

So, the prototype is quietly grandfathered in, the governance process is declared a success ("See? We caught nothing!"), and everyone moves on to the next 18-month approval queue.

Wordsmithing: The Sweetest Form of Torture

For every new buzzword that enters the lexicon, agentic, multimodal, retrieval-augmented, chain-of-thought, constitutional AI, immediately commission a full manuscript of guidelines.

Not a one-pager. A 42-page living document. With version history. With tracked changes. With comments from seventeen different functions.

Then begin the sacred ritual of wordsmithing.

Change "should consider" to "must give due regard to." Change "high risk" to "elevated concern level." Change "as appropriate" to "commensurate with the contextually determined materiality threshold."

Each edit must be debated in committee. Each debate must

produce minutes. Each set of minutes must be approved at the next meeting.

Months pass. The document grows. The technology moves on.

Meanwhile, real work is quietly done in shadow channels where no one is foolish enough to ask for governance approval.

The Autobahn vs. Bangalore / Jakarta Analogy

Imagine the German Autobahn: clear rules, posted limits only where genuinely needed, drivers who understand both the freedom and the responsibility. You can floor your Bugatti at 220 km/h because everyone knows the rules, trusts the system, and accepts that speed comes with accountability.

Now imagine driving in Bangalore or Jakarta, two wonderful, chaotic, life-affirming cities where traffic is an official form of performance art. Lanes are theoretical. Indicators are decorative. Right of way is negotiated through eye contact, horn duration, and sheer audacity. Rules exist, but they are applied subjectively, inconsistently, when convenient, noticeable, or when someone is bothered enough to enforce them.

Who in their right mind would want to deploy AI the way one drives on the Autobahn, clear rules, predictable enforcement, freedom within boundaries? That would allow actual progress. That would allow innovation at speed.

No. We want gloriously subjective, magnificently inconsistent, emotionally exhausting governance. Only then can you be sure nothing dangerous (i.e., useful) will ever reach production too quickly.

OSS Wisdom of the Day

When we created the Fairness, Ethics, Accountability and Transparency (FEAT) principles, arguably laying some of the earliest foundations for modern AI governance. We deliberately kept it to one page with 14 simple principles.

Idiots. What were we thinking… the opportunity we missed for marvellous, insufferable complexity!

"Advocate 'caution'. Be 'reasonable' and urge your fellow-conferees to be 'reasonable' and avoid haste which might result in embarrassments or difficulties later on." — Simple Sabotage Field Manual, 1944

So go ahead. Layer the committees. Multiply the standards. Wordsmith until the language itself surrenders. Turn governance into performance art.

The innovation will suffocate quietly in the dark.

The Page Is Left Intentionally Blank

It's just a flesh wound! (The AI model said, right before hallucinating the entire quarterly forecast.)

4 POLISH THE SYMPTOMS, PRESERVE THE ISSUE – WHY FIXING THE OBVIOUS ITCHES FEELS SO MUCH MORE PRODUCTIVE THAN EVER TOUCHING THE ROOT CAUSES

"Insanity is doing the same thing over and over again and expecting different results."

— often attributed to Albert Einstein (whether he said it or not hardly matters; the line lands like a brick through the window of every transformation programme still running the same playbook from 2018)

We are all in a crazy simulation, perhaps. Or perhaps we are just very good at pretending the rules haven't changed while continuing to play by the old ones. Either way, the outcome is the same: we keep doing what we have always done, only faster, shinier, and with more tokens per second. And when the results are still disappointing, we do it again. Harder. With more committees. With more rebrands. With more hope.

Welcome to the third act of the tragedy.

Chapter 1 taught you never to ask "why".

Chapter 2 taught you how to suffocate anything that accidentally survives asking "why" by wrapping it in governance so thick it can no longer breathe.

Chapter 3 is where the survivors, those few half-dead pilots that somehow made it through the gauntlet, get lovingly polished, tweaked, and bandaged… while the underlying issue is left to quietly metastasise.

Because treating the rash feels so much more productive than admitting there might be something far uglier underneath.

The Comfort of Visible Fixes

By this point you have a small number of pilots that have escaped governance purgatory. They are fragile, compromised, over-engineered, and barely fit for purpose. But they exist. They have demos. They have metrics (mostly vanity). They have slides.

So, what do we do next? We fix what is visibly broken.

The data is dirty? Clean one dataset for the pilot. The legacy workflow is clunky? Bolt a shiny new AI layer on top like a Christmas decoration on a dying tree. The handoffs between teams are painful? Add middleware, another integration, a notification bot, a dashboard that shows the handoff is still painful but now in real time.

We stay busy. We look action-oriented. We produce progress reports with green status indicators.

Nobody asks why the data became dirty in the first place. Nobody asks why the workflow is still running on logic from the Clinton administration. Nobody asks why the handoffs are painful when the organisation chart was last redrawn in 2019.

Because asking those questions would mean looking under the bed. And under the bed are gory monsters: siloed incentives, misaligned KPIs, decades of technical debt, decision rights that no longer match reality, and a culture that rewards looking busy more than being effective.

Far easier to polish the symptoms.

AI as the Universal Band-Aid

Here is the subtle genius of this phase.

While the level of expectation for AI is higher than the Eiffel Tower, we consciously ignore that the standards on the similar BAU process which AI is meant to augment or replace is perhaps as solid as an elephant walk on a tightrope.

We demand near-perfection from AI outputs while happily tolerating mediocrity in the very BAU processes AI is supposed to improve. We expect AI to work around broken processes instead of requiring us to redesign them. We fix symptoms in one silo without ever looking at the end-to-end system.

We never go back to the connected network validity. We never revisit the individual equations to see if they still make sense when assembled into a unified optimisation problem. We certainly never admit that the entire hypothesis might be flawed.

If the outcome still doesn't achieve the desired objective? Just keep pushing. Add more compute. Fine-tune harder. Prompt harder. Never, ever go back to understand those gory monsters under the bed.

Failure Guidebook Technique #1 – Lift-and-Shift

Perfection The fastest way to magnify every flaw in the old process is to simply "lift and shift" it into the AI era. Treat AI as a magic overlay rather than a reason to redesign. Garbage in, garbage out on steroids. Broken handoffs? AI will just make them faster and more expensive. Bad data? AI will confidently hallucinate on top of it. Legacy logic from 1998? AI will execute it at lightning speed… still wrong. Do this consistently and you will achieve the rare feat of making a bad process look even worse while spending millions in the process.

Failure Guidebook Technique #2 – Baseline Blindness Never, ever establish a rigorous baseline measurement of the current BAU process before layering AI on top. Why would you? Baselines are depressing. They show how slow, error-prone, and expensive the current state really is. They create uncomfortable context. They make improvement harder to fake.

Instead, start from a vague sense of "it's bad" and then declare any small lift a massive win. "Before AI we took three days to process invoices. Now it takes two and a half!" Never mind that the three days were caused by manual re-keying between two incompatible systems that nobody has fixed in fifteen years. Green status achieved. Next pilot, please.

Failure Guidebook Technique #3 – Edge-Case Amnesia Design the system around the happy path. Ignore the long tail of exceptions until they appear in production. When they do, add more humans to "supervise" rather than redesign the process so exceptions are rare or handled automatically. This ensures AI remains a shiny but brittle ornament rather than a genuine replacement or augmentation.

The Continuum Problem

AI is not a thing. It is a continuum. It flows through every part of the organisation like Q pestering Captain Picard, annoyingly marvellous, endlessly charming, and constantly forcing you to confront the limits of your own understanding.

Data was always a continuum too, but data never had Q's charisma. Data was relegated to the forgotten background, treated as plumbing. AI, on the other hand, arrives with fireworks and existential stakes. It refuses to stay in the background. It cuts straight to the heart of the traditionally verticalized organisation.

And yet we still treat it like a vertical project. A thing to be governed. A thing to be piloted. A thing to be measured in tokens per second.

We never ask whether the continuum itself demands a different operating model.

The Quiet Tragedy

The pilots keep running. The dashboards keep glowing green. The leadership keeps getting updated slides with upward-trending curves.

Meanwhile the issue spreads.

The data stays dirty except for the one dataset someone polished for the demo. The legacy workflows stay broken except where the AI duct-tape holds them together. The handoffs stay painful except where someone built a notification bot to remind everyone how painful they are.

And when the outcome still doesn't arrive, we do what we have always done: We do the same thing again. Only this time with more layers. More wordsmithing. More committees. More hope.

Because hope is free. And insanity is doing the same thing over and over again and expecting different results.

So, keep polishing the symptoms. Keep ignoring the issue. Keep treating the itches as if they were the problem.

It feels productive. It looks busy. It buys time.

And time is the only currency left when you have already decided never to ask why.

"So long, and thanks for all the fish." — Douglas Adams

5 NOTHING SCREWS UP A TRANSFORMATION QUITE LIKE LETTING THE TECH GODS DECIDE WHAT THE MERE MORTALS ACTUALLY NEED

Congratulations, dear reader. You've just green-lit the ultimate failure formula. You've gathered your brightest minds, allocated a war chest that would make Silicon Valley blush, and here's the masterstroke, handed the entire AI kingdom over to Technology. Not as humble enablers of the business, mind you. No. As the exalted owners and high priests of everything from prompt engineering to "strategic vision."

You actually get two distinct flavours of danger, each lethal in its own special way.

First, the **CIO Dungeon**: the land of ERP integration, security reviews, infrastructure stability, compliance checkboxes, and the sacred duty of "keeping the lights on." Everything must be centralised, governed, and made "enterprise ready." Business requests are politely filtered through 17 layers of architecture and risk assessments because "we can't have shadow solutions."

Then there's the **CTO Ivory Tower**: where the really smart people live. They explore bleeding-edge technologies that are certainly too advanced for the business. With the ferocious pace of AI evolution, the CTO office can comfortably keep every promising idea in permanent "proof-of-concept," "incubation," or "exploratory" status for years. After all, by the time it's ready for production, there will be something even newer and shinier to chase.

Of course, the CEO deserves a quiet round of applause too. After reading about AI in the in-flight magazine, the simplest and most decisive move was to toss the article to Technology with the transformative instruction: "Figure it out." Strategic delegation at its finest.

Then came Generative AI. And oh, the delicious irony. Suddenly Jane from Marketing and John from Operations discovered they could do genuinely useful things with nothing more than GenAI in their browser. Jane knocked out surprisingly good campaign copy and customer emails in minutes. John built a quick agent that summarised supplier emails and flagged delays. Both looked at the polished internal PoCs their IT colleagues were promising after six months of "enterprise readiness" and thought: "Wait… mine already works better than that."

This is where the sabotage truly sings. The business now expects the internal GenAI products to have the same effortless polish and instant usefulness as the consumer tools they use every day. After all, if a motivated person with no IT help can spin up a convincing PoC in an afternoon using public models, why does the official version need eighteen governance gates, three architecture reviews, and a six-month roadmap? The gap between consumer magic and enterprise reality becomes the silent killer of momentum, and the perfect excuse for Technology to explain why "it's more complicated than that."

Treating AI as just another infrastructure project was never the sole cause of past AI winters, but it certainly helped. The technology was brittle, the over-promising was epic, and the organisational reflex was always the same: put it safely in the dungeon or the tower where it could be properly "managed", away from messy things like customers and revenue.

Technology has long outpaced the convenient organisational fiction that the teams charged with keeping the lights on or chasing the bleeding edge are the ideal home for genuinely business-transformational AI. Ironically, the organisations whose primary job is stability and security are often the worst possible owners of something that actually requires speed, experimentation, and constant course correction.

The Technology Formula for Success (i.e. Failure) To achieve maximum dysfunction, follow this simple playbook:

1. Declare that all AI initiatives must be centrally governed and delivered through Technology "for consistency and control."
2. Insist that every use case must go through the central platform, the central data lake, the central governance board, and the central security review.
3. Measure success by technical metrics: model accuracy, tokens per second, deployment velocity, and infrastructure cost optimization.
4. Quietly deprioritize (or completely ignore) business outcomes such as incremental revenue, customer satisfaction lift, or cost-to-serve reduction.
5. When the business complains that the central platform is too slow, too rigid, or doesn't solve their actual problem, respond with: "You need to work within the enterprise architecture." Then, to really seal the deal, set up another committee to

"unblock" the issue.

Pro Tips & Saboteur Guidance

The Enterprise Architecture Purity Cult Treat any deviation from the sacred enterprise architecture as heresy. Insist that even the simplest chatbot must conform to 47 enterprise standards before it can be piloted. This ensures nothing useful ever sees the light of day.

The Security-First, Business-Second Doctrine Lead with "security and compliance" as the primary filter for every idea. When the business asks for speed, reply solemnly: "We cannot compromise on security." This is an unbeatable conversation stopper.

The One Ring to Rule Them All Platform Strategy Declare that there shall be only one unified AI platform to rule them all. Force every department to use it, regardless of whether it actually solves their problem. When it inevitably fails to meet specific needs, blame the business for not adapting to the platform.

The Roadmap Over Results Religion Spend months building beautiful multi-year roadmaps full of impressive milestones. Measure progress by how many roadmap items have been "planned" rather than by any actual value delivered. Roadmaps are comforting. Results are risky.

Timeline Worship (The Holy Date Doctrine) Above all, treat the agreed release date as sacred scripture. When the date inevitably slips, never admit it was because the scope was unrealistic or the governance layers too thick. Instead, point elegantly at compliance, security, or "additional risk reviews that were unfortunately required." This sacred ritual allows Technology to maintain the appearance of control while quietly extending every timeline by 40–60%. The business learns that complaining about delays is futile, the new date is simply "the new baseline." Repeat until hope expires.

The Bleeding-Edge Forever Strategy (CTO Special) Keep every promising AI capability in "exploratory" or "incubation" status indefinitely. When the business asks when it will be ready, reply with calm wisdom: "The technology is still maturing." This works especially well because AI is always maturing.

Keep repeating the sacred mantra: "We are a tech company with a banking license / retail license / healthcare license / [insert delusion here]."

Marvel at your own infrastructure. Measure success by model accuracy and deployment velocity. Watch in slow-motion horror as the business quietly builds shadow AI agents in whatever they can because waiting for the governance deck (or the latest unblocking committee) was too painful.

Celebrate when your multimillion-dollar "AI platform" achieves 99.9% uptime… while delivering precisely zero incremental customer delight or EBITDA.

The forward-looking provocation is this: in the age of ubiquitous, conversational intelligence, AI is no longer purely a technology initiative. It is a business operating model. The organisations that thrive will be the ones where the tone and direction are set horizontally by the people who own the customer, the P&L, and the messy reality of value creation.

Technology has a critical supporting role, ensuring security, reliability, scalability, and protecting the business from the very real risks of customer-facing AI gone wrong. But that role must be servant, not owner.

So, by all means, keep AI firmly in the technology organisation. Install more governance. Demand more roadmaps. Glorify the platform above all else. Set up more unblocking committees. Worship the timeline like its holy writ.

It's the surest, most elegant way to screw it all up.

And if, heaven forbid, one of your technology leaders reads this and decides to take that humble backseat anyway… well, we'll just have to write a sequel titled "How to Survive When Your Engineers Start Listening to the Business."

6 NO ONE IS ACCOUNTABLE & EVERYONE IS A CO-HEAD – BECAUSE NOTHING SCREAMS "SPEED OF AI" LIKE REQUIRING CONSENSUS FROM SIX BUSY PEOPLE BEFORE LUNCH

Imagine this.

Someone in the room finally says the words everyone has been avoiding for months: "We need clear accountability for this AI transformation."

The silence lasts exactly 2.3 seconds.

Then, like a well-rehearsed dance, the group springs into action. Within ten minutes they have appointed six co-heads, four co-leads, two "strategic alignment facilitators," one "accountability working group," and a brand-new "cross-functional ownership task force" to define what accountability actually means.

Welcome to the accountability black hole, the place where responsibility goes to die a slow, painful, committee-approved death.

The Co-Head Hydra

The most reliable way to ensure no one is ever truly accountable is to make sure **everyone** is a little bit accountable.

Replace any single owner with a glorious hydra of co-heads, co-champions, and dotted-line matrices. When something goes wrong, blame simply diffuses like cheap coffee in a big meeting.

Failure Guidebook Technique #1 – The Hydra Principle When in doubt, add more heads. If one co-head isn't enough, make it three. If three isn't enough, create a "Steering Committee of Co-Heads." The more heads, the harder it is to find the neck.

With all the co-heads in the room, no one truly knows who does what. This is particularly beneficial when intermixed with locking AI in the CIO dungeon or CTO ivory tower, the tech team continues as they please, while the business co-heads spend their days in alignment syncs wondering whose job it actually is.

The Hive-Mind Collective

Never let a single person make a clear decision. Instead, turn every decision into a beautiful, endless hive-mind consensus process.

Require "alignment syncs," "pre-alignment syncs," and "alignment sync retrospectives." Make sure the final decision is so thoroughly collective that when it inevitably fails, no individual can be blamed.

Failure Guidebook Technique #2 – The Collective Shield If everyone is responsible, then magically, no one is responsible. When things go south, simply say: "This was a collective decision." The beauty is that "collective" is impossible to fire.

This is also excellent training ground for future government officials. The skills developed here, mastering the art of looking busy while achieving nothing, crafting perfectly vague language, and ensuring nothing ever quite lands on one person's desk, are directly transferable to public sector work.

Always Blame the Previous Person

This is a classic that never gets old.

Failure Guidebook Technique #3 – The Previous Regime Defence When anything goes wrong, immediately point to the person who is no longer in the room. "The previous leadership set unrealistic targets." "This was inherited from the old strategy." "They didn't understand AI."

The predecessor becomes the ultimate scapegoat, conveniently unavailable for comment.

The Risk of Doing vs. Not Doing

Create a quiet (sometimes loud) culture where the risk of doing something is always greater than the risk of doing nothing.

Propose a change? Risk being labelled "not aligned." Take a decision? Risk being wrong. Stay silent, attend every meeting, nod at the right moments, and you will be praised for "strong execution" and "cultural fit."

Doing nothing becomes the smartest career strategy in the room.

Failure Guidebook Technique #4 – The Inaction

Reward System Design performance scorecards that reward "collaboration," "strategic participation," and "thoughtful alignment" rather than actual outcomes. The person who speaks the most in meetings but never decides anything often ends up with the highest rating.

The Sacred Exception: The Fall Guy

And if, God forbid, someone actually steps forward and tries to be accountable?

Make sure they are either accountable **to the hydra** (so their decision can be immediately diluted by six other co-heads) or they are held accountable **for the failure** (so everyone else can point at them and say "See? We told you it was risky").

This is the perfect catch-22. The only person who ever takes real accountability is the one who gets blamed when it inevitably goes wrong.

The Quiet Tragedy

In the end, you have built something truly remarkable: An organisation where everyone is busy, no one is accountable, and the transformation slowly dies of diffusion.

Decisions evaporate into perpetual alignment syncs. Blame diffuses into thin air. Progress becomes optional. And everyone can honestly say they "did their part."

Welcome to the accountability black hole. Population: everyone. Accountability: zero.

7 PROMISE THE MOON, DELIVER THE POWERPOINT – HOW TO OVERHYPE AI TO THE BOARD UNTIL CREDIBILITY DIES IN PRODUCTION

There comes a sacred moment in every AI transformation.

It usually happens in a brightly lit boardroom, after the coffee has gone cold and the initial excitement has settled into a comfortable haze. Someone leans forward, clears their throat, and with the gravest possible expression declares:

"We are going to transform the company with AI."

A gentle ripple of nods goes around the table. Eyes light up. The future suddenly feels within reach.

This is the precise moment the hype machine is switched on at full power, and the sabotage reaches its most elegant form.

You have inherited ambitious revenue targets, aggressive cost/income ratio improvements, and lofty operational efficiency goals. Whether these ambitions are realistic or were simply set based on the direction of the wind last year is almost beside the point. Because now you have the ultimate get-out-of-jail-free card: AI.

AI is the literal messiah that will make these targets "just happen." Of course.

New-age companies born without any legacy dinosaurs have achieved mind-spinning results with AI. They can do it, so surely, we can too. Never mind that those companies started from a clean sheet of paper while you are carrying decades of technical debt, misaligned incentives, and processes designed before the internet existed.

Failure Guidebook Technique #1 – The Aspirational Moonshot Set financial goals that would require near-perfect (99%+) accuracy and flawless execution. When the folks trying to implement meekly try to voice that "AI doesn't actually work that way," simply bang the table and declare: "The savings/revenue have already been committed in the budget! You have to achieve it!"

The board loves bold targets. The CFO has already baked them into next year's plan. The only thing left is for AI to magically deliver.

To show how serious you are, schedule lots and lots of workshops. Invite as many people as possible. Fill the calendar with sessions on strategy, use cases, ethics, agentic AI, and how to run even more workshops. The more workshops, the more serious the transformation looks.

Failure Guidebook Technique #2 – The New-Age Envy Point to the shiny successes of younger, nimbler companies and say: "Look at what they're doing with AI. If they can transform overnight, so can we."

Even when some brave soul timidly acknowledges that "maybe we are a little more complex" and "it isn't as easy," the expectation remains exactly the same. The outcomes and benefits should still arrive as if circumstances had no correlation whatsoever with reality, especially when hope is high and budget targets have already been committed.

Failure Guidebook Technique #3 – The Board's Laser Pointer Feed Provide the Board with sufficiently exciting yet sufficiently confusing information to keep the laser pointer moving at an optimal speed. Present beautiful hockey-stick projections, impressive technical metrics, and the occasional mention of "agentic capabilities." Mix in just enough jargon to sound sophisticated, but not so much that questions become unavoidable. When concern about risk surfaces, acknowledge it solemnly ("We take security and compliance extremely seriously") while immediately pivoting back to the upside ("which is why we are moving with appropriate urgency").

When executed correctly, the Board will leave energised, slightly worried, and fully committed to the next round of workshops and budget increases.

Failure Guidebook Technique #4 – Introduce Fresh Buzzwords Sprinkle in exciting new terminology like "Agentic AI." Because obviously we have never had agents operating inside a company before. The board will nod approvingly at the sophistication. The implementers will quietly sigh.

The presentation is beautiful. The slides are full of hockey-stick growth curves. Everyone leaves feeling that the future is finally within reach.

Then reality shows up.

Most organizations discover (usually around month nine) that the promised 15–30% cost reduction or 20% revenue uplift was based on optimistic assumptions, perfect data, and zero resistance from the existing organisation. In practice, the actual impact is closer to "we saved three hours a week in one department" or "the model is 87% accurate on a very narrow slice of cases."

But by then the savings have already been committed in the budget. The headcount reduction targets have been announced to investors. The new revenue numbers are baked into the guidance.

So, what do you do? You move the goalposts, rebrand the pilot as a "learning experience," and create a new slide deck titled "AI Journey Update – On Track for Strategic Value Realisation."

Failure Guidebook Technique #5 – The Credibility Canyon When the gap between the town-hall vision and the actual P&L impact becomes impossible to ignore, simply announce that "we are shifting from pilot mode to scaled value capture" and promise even bigger results next quarter.

Reports from leading consultancies quietly confirm what many are experiencing: despite hundreds of billions invested globally, only a tiny fraction of organisations report any meaningful bottom-line impact from AI. But none of that matters in the boardroom. Because the slides still look fantastic.

And that, dear reader, is the true art of the PowerPoint transformation.

Promise the moon. Deliver the PowerPoint. Repeat until credibility quietly dies in production.

8 MEASURE EVERYTHING EXCEPT WHAT MATTERS – ROC CURVES, TOKENS PER SECOND, AND OTHER IRRELEVANT VANITY METRICS THAT LET YOU LOOK BUSY WHILE VALUE EVAPORATES

There's nothing quite like the warm glow of a beautiful dashboard.

Green numbers trending upward. Impressive accuracy percentages. Latency graphs that look like they were designed by Apple. Token-per-second counters that make everyone in the room feel like they're part of something revolutionary.

This is the moment when the transformation feels like it's working.

Never mind that none of these numbers have anything to do with actual money, customers, or competitive advantage. The important thing is that they look good in the quarterly review.

Welcome to the wonderful world of vanity metrics, where

you can be technically brilliant and commercially irrelevant at the same time.

The Sacred Art of Measuring the Wrong Things

The golden rule of this phase is simple: measure everything that is easy to measure and ignore everything that actually matters.

Failure Guidebook Technique #1 – The Vanity Dashboard Celebrate model accuracy, inference latency, cost per token, number of prompts processed, and governance compliance rates. Put them on big, colourful dashboards with upward arrows and smiley-face emojis. When someone asks about incremental revenue or cost-to-serve reduction, reply with a confident: "We're still in the optimisation phase. These are leading indicators."

The board will nod approvingly. After all, the graphs look very professional.

Failure Guidebook Technique #2 – The 99.9% Uptime Celebration Achieve 99.9% uptime on your central AI platform and throw a small internal party. Ignore the fact that the platform is delivering precisely zero meaningful business outcomes. High-five the team. Send an all-hands email titled "Another Milestone Achieved!" Meanwhile, the business quietly continues using spreadsheets and shadow tools because the official platform is too slow or too restricted to be useful.

Cost Without Context

Tokens per second does give you an indication of cost, and cost does have merit. But what does cost actually tell you if it cannot be combined with a downstream impact?

Answering the question "What does this cost give me?" is

the part that gets conveniently skipped. You can proudly report that you reduced inference cost by 40%, but if that saving comes from a model that is being used for something that adds no value to the customer or the business, you have simply become more efficient at wasting money.

Failure Guidebook Technique #3 – The Cost-Without-Value Trap Measure cost per token religiously. Celebrate every reduction. Never link it back to a tangible business outcome. When someone asks, "What value did we get for those cheaper tokens?", reply: "That's a downstream question. We're focused on optimization here."

This allows you to feel extremely responsible while delivering zero incremental value.

The "Not the Only Stakeholder" Defence

When a particular business unit dares to complain that the central platform isn't delivering value for them, the standard response is elegant:

"That business is not the only stakeholder."

This line is pure magic. It implies that the needs of the wider organisation (i.e., the central team's preferences) must take precedence. It creates a beautiful perception of acceptability: "Yes, your use case might not be working, but the overall governance framework is healthy."

Failure Guidebook Technique #4 – The Stakeholder Diffusion When any individual business pushes back, remind them they are not the only stakeholder. This ensures that no single unit's pain is ever allowed to disrupt the grand central vision. The result? Everyone is slightly unhappy, but the central team can claim the system is "balanced."

The Quiet Tragedy

The organizations that master this phase become truly world-class at one thing: Looking extremely busy while achieving almost nothing of value.

They have dashboards that would make a NASA engineer jealous. They have KPIs so numerous that no one can remember them all. They have weekly reports that take longer to read than the actual work they're supposed to measure.

And yet the P&L barely moves.

OSS Wisdom of the Day

"Work slowly. Be as clumsy and inaccurate as possible." — Simple Sabotage Field Manual, 1944

So, keep measuring everything except what matters. Fill your walls with glowing screens. Celebrate every technical milestone. And when someone gently asks, "But how is this helping the business?", simply point to the beautiful upward trend and say:

"We're optimising."

The room will nod. The meeting will end. The value will continue to evaporate, beautifully tracked, perfectly documented, and entirely missing.

CHAPTER 9: ARE WE THE BADDIES? – HOW TO TURN YOUR ENTIRE AI "TRANSFORMATION" INTO A QUIETLY AUTHORITARIAN NIGHTMARE

Imagine walking into a workplace where rules designed to create "responsible AI" end up feeling like invisible bars, where asking honest questions about value sometimes leads to polite defensiveness rather than discussion, and where talented colleagues quietly update their résumés while the official transformation deck still glows green.

These experiences are not rare anomalies. They are the natural outcome when good intentions drift toward toxic control.

Frank Dikötter's study of dictatorships shows how authoritarian systems take root: power centralised amid crisis with promises of salvation, authority placed above messy reality, loyalty prized over competence, information tightly controlled, fear and surveillance dressed up as "governance," and ideology bent to justify every new layer of process. These features form a self-sustaining cycle: fear ensures compliance, compliance simulates devotion, and the structure holds until reality intervenes.

Nations change slowly, bound by armies and history. Organisations? They can turn on a dime.

What starts as sensible structure to "tame the risks of AI" often solidifies into something far more rigid. A fast-growing company, tired of early chaos, sets firm policies only to watch them become inflexible edicts that ignore real-life context. HR, aiming to reduce risk, expands reporting channels and approval layers that later serve as tools for self-protection. Decision rights grow deliciously hazy in pursuit of "alignment," so no one is quite sure who truly owns outcomes. Accountability appears assigned but is often purely performative. The named "responsible" person simply carries out instructions from the hidden power centre.

Teams stop asking "What's the right path for the business?" and start asking, "What will please the governance committee?" This breeds inefficiency, suspicion, silos, and a quiet cult of personality around those who control the approval flows. The organisation begins to value navigation skills, reading the room, signalling loyalty, mastering the jargon, over actual merit or customer impact.

Failure Guidebook Technique #1 – Never Revise the KPIs Keep the old revenue targets and headcount-reduction goals sacred. Never, ever revisit them. When someone timidly suggests "Maybe these numbers are no longer realistic given what we've learned," reply with a gentle smile: "We're not here to lower the bar. We're here to raise our game with AI."

The KPIs become holy writ. Everyone quietly knows they're fantasy, but no one dares say it out loud. Doing nothing about the targets is rewarded far more than the risky act of updating them.

Failure Guidebook Technique #2 – Reward Inaction Over Action Create an environment where the safest career move is to do nothing. Propose a change? Risk being labelled "not aligned." Suggest revising a process? Risk being told "that's not in scope." Stay quiet, attend the meetings, nod at the right moments, and you'll be praised for "strong execution" and "cultural fit."

The message becomes crystal clear: the risk of doing something is always greater than the risk of doing nothing. So, people stop doing things.

Failure Guidebook Technique #3 – Turn Change Agents into Compliance Agents Never guide or protect real change agents. Instead, quietly convert them. Give them titles like "AI Transformation Lead" or "Responsible AI Champion." Then drown them in governance templates, risk matrices, and alignment workshops until their job is no longer to drive change but to police it.

The best change agents either burn out or become the most effective guardians of the status quo. Either way, you win.

Failure Guidebook Technique #4 – Make Proposing Change Dangerous Build a quiet (sometimes not-so-quiet) culture where anyone who suggests a real change is viewed with suspicion. "That's not aligned with our responsible AI principles." "We need to take this to the next governance review." "We should probably form a working group first."

The fear is subtle but powerful: the personal and professional risk of proposing something new is far higher than the risk of keeping things exactly as they are. So, people stop proposing.

In one organization, a blanket "no exceptions" stance on AI tool usage was rolled out to ensure equity and compliance. When genuine business needs or personal experimentation arose, even strong contributors faced unyielding enforcement. Frustration built. Key talent left. Morale suffered as people felt their humanity (and their ability to get work done) was secondary to policy purity.

In another setting, performance evaluations increasingly highlighted "alignment with the AI strategy" and "cultural fit with responsible AI principles" above quantifiable achievements. Employees who delivered solid results but offered thoughtful pushback on the central platform found themselves overlooked for advancement, while those who consistently echoed the party line rose. Over time, the culture tilted toward visible agreement rather than independent thinking, quietly driving away the very voices that once drove innovation.

These stories are not fiction. They mirror real experiences shared in anonymous employee feedback across the industry.

Most leaders do not set out to create fear. They aim to safeguard progress, learn from past stumbles, and impose order on complexity. Yet inherited or evolved systems can subtly favour compliance, sideline dissent, and foster reliance. Psychological safety fades. Creativity slows. Independent thinkers depart, leaving a more uniform but less vibrant group that confuses allegiance with excellence.

This recalls the sharp sketch from That Mitchell and Webb Look, where two officers notice the skull emblems on their uniforms and one quietly mutter, "Are we the baddies?"

The line lands because the realisation comes after the system has normalised itself.

So, by all means, keep centralising. Prize alignment over achievement. Enforce blanket rules with zero exceptions. Demand visible harmony. Never revise the KPIs. Reward doing nothing. Make proposing change dangerous. Turn change agents into compliance agents.

Turn your AI transformation into a quietly authoritarian nightmare while sincerely believing you're doing it for the people, for the culture, and for "responsible innovation."

It's the surest, most elegant way to watch psychological safety evaporate, creativity slow to a crawl, and your best people quietly update their résumés, all while your governance deck remains beautifully green.

The room will nod. The meeting will end. The innovation will suffocate quietly in the dark… and you can comfort yourself that at least everyone meant well.

The Page Is Left Intentionally Blank

One day, son, all this blank space will be yours. Just like the value from our last pilot.

EPILOGUE: THE FINAL SABOTAGE – OR HOW TO KEEP THE LIGHTS OFF WHILE CLAIMING THE FUTURE IS BRIGHT

And so, we reach the end of our little field manual.

If you have read this far, you now possess a complete set of time-tested techniques for ensuring that even the most promising AI transformation collapses under the weight of its own elegance. You know how to begin without asking why, how to strangle momentum with governance, how to polish symptoms while the issue thrives, how to park the whole endeavour safely with technology, how to diffuse accountability until no one can be blamed, how to over-promise to the board with just the right mixture of excitement and confusion, how to measure everything except anything that actually matters, and finally how to turn good intentions into quietly authoritarian control, all while sincerely believing you were protecting the organization and its people.

The real genius of these methods is that none of them require malice. They require only the ordinary, everyday habits of modern corporate life: the love of committees, the comfort of roadmaps, the safety of never quite deciding, the quiet relief of blaming the previous regime, and the irresistible urge to appear busy while avoiding anything that might actually move the needle.

The *Simple Sabotage Field Manual* of 1944 taught ordinary citizens how to cripple organizations through small, persistent acts of organized incompetence. Eighty-two years later, we have refined those techniques into something far more sophisticated. We no longer need enemy agents. We do it to ourselves, enthusiastically, with PowerPoint decks, workshops, and perfectly worded governance documents.

If, after reading these pages, you have recognized your own organization in more than one chapter… congratulations. You are now dangerously close to success. The first step toward avoiding these elegant disasters is admitting you have been practicing them with commendable consistency, even if unintentionally.

The second step is simpler still: stop.

Put down the laser pointer. Skip the next workshop. Ask the awkward question nobody wants to hear. Accept that technology advancement has long outpaced the structures we keep forcing it into. Let the business set the tone and let technology do what it does best. Serve, not rule.

Or, of course, you can do none of those things. You can close this handbook, schedule another alignment sync, update the roadmap, and prepare the next beautiful set of slides.

The choice, as always, is yours.

Just remember to carry a towel.

You never know when you might need to put it over your head.

ABOUT THE AUTHOR

Dr. D.R. Hardoon is a mildly confused human who spends most of his time trying to understand why people do the things they do. He is an enthusiastic (though mediocre) bird watcher, a reluctant gym attendee, and a firm believer that the meaning of life is probably hiding somewhere between the 42nd and 43rd attempt at making decent sourdough bread.

He has been known to stare at spreadsheets for hours, not because he enjoys them, but because he finds the patterns strangely comforting. He still hasn't figured out how to fold a fitted sheet properly, which he considers one of life's great unsolved mysteries.

He lives with the quiet hope that one day he will understand both birds and humans. So far, the birds are winning.

On a Serious Note,

If you have made it this far, you will have noticed that this handbook is written with a generous helping of dark humour, irony, and deliberate exaggeration. The satirical tone is intentional.

On a more serious note, the patterns and "failure recipes" described in these pages are drawn from more than two decades of collective hands-on experience in data, advanced analytics, and artificial intelligence. This journey has spanned research, regulatory authorities, financial institutions, and technology-driven organisations across Asia and beyond.

The frustrations, ironies, and repeated missteps catalogued in this book are therefore not the story of any single organisation or any single individual, but an aggregate of stories observed across many years and many different environments. They reflect systemic challenges that continue to appear with impressive consistency across industries, geographies, and company sizes.

My sincere hope is that by naming these failure modes with affection and precision, and by encouraging you to laugh at them, this handbook might help current and future leaders avoid at least some of the more elegant traps that have claimed so many well-intentioned AI initiatives.

The mirror is offered with respect, and with the genuine belief that we can, and should, do better.

- Dr. David R. Hardoon

www.davidroihardoon.com

Made in the USA
Coppell, TX
22 June 2026

82921211R00036